C.1

E
HOG

Hogrogian, Nonny.

The cat who loved
to sing

JUN 30 1988

$13.99   f

	DATE		
OC 29 '90			
NOV 1 4 1990			
NOV 14.1990			
OC1 8 00			

© THE BAKER & TAYLOR CO.

THE CAT WHO LOVED TO SING

THE CAT WHO LOVED TO SING

By Nonny Hogrogian

ALFRED A. KNOPF ·❦· NEW YORK

THIS IS A BORZOI BOOK PUBLISHED BY ALFRED A. KNOPF, INC.

Library of Congress Cataloging-in-Publication Data
Hogrogian, Nonny. The cat who loved to sing.
Summary: A cat who loves to sing trades one thing for another until he
finally gains a mandolin.
[1. Cats—Fiction] I. Title.
PZ7.H6844Cat   1988   [E]   86-27358
ISBN 0-394-89004-3   ISBN 0-394-99004-8 (lib. bdg.)

FOR MICHAEL HEDGE WHO LOVES TO FISH

There once was a cat who loved to sing,
trala lala lala.

One day he was singing along
as he romped down a wooded path,
and suddenly he stepped on a thorn.
"Ow! Ow ow ow ow ow!" he cried,
and hopped along in pain.
"What ails you, poor cat?"
called a woman from her garden.
She put down her basket
and pulled out the thorn and said,
"What a fine needle this would make."

So she offered the cat some freshly baked bread
in return for the useful thorn.
"I gladly accept," said the cat,
"and thank you for your help."
And he went on his way down the wooded path
with the bread tucked under his arm.

Trala lala
I gave my thorn and got some bread
that I will eat with a succulent mouse.
Trala lala lala

A fox was running through the woods
with a hen he had snatched from a neighboring farm.
When he noticed the cat and smelled the fine loaf,
a thought came into his head.
"Think of *all* the fat chickens
I could lure with that bread—
certainly more than this one lonely hen."

So the fox jumped out and blocked the way
and offered the hen in return for the bread.

The cat gave up the bread
and accepted the hen
and continued on his way.

Trala lala
I gave my thorn and got some bread.
I lost the bread and gained a hen.
How tasty it will be.
Trala

The cat traveled on and he met a young bride.
"What a wonderful hen
you are holding," she said.
"It would make a fine treat for my husband's supper.
Will you trade it for some nice red yarn?"
"Yes, of course," said the cat.
And he gave the hen to the bride
in return for her yarn.

Trala lala
I gave my thorn and got some bread.
I lost the bread and gained a hen.
I gave the hen for some nice red yarn.
Trala lala lala

Just then an old woman came hobbling by.
"How lucky I am," she said.
"I was going to town to buy some yarn,
but I see that you have the perfect color.
Won't you accept this fine old coat
in exchange for that beautiful yarn?"
The cat agreed to the trade
and continued on his way.

Trala lala
I gave my thorn and got some bread.
I lost the bread and gained a hen.
I gave the hen for some nice red yarn.
I traded the yarn for a fine old coat.
Trala lala lala

He passed an old man in need of a coat.
"You may have my dog," the old man said,
"since I can hardly feed myself."
"A dog!" exclaimed the cat.
"I never dreamed of owning a dog!
But I haven't made a bad trade yet.
Yes, I will take your dog."
And he continued down the path.

Trala lala
I gave my thorn and got some bread.
I lost the bread and gained a hen.
I gave the hen for some nice red yarn.
I traded the yarn for a fine old coat.
I gave the coat for this scruffy dog.
Trala lala lala

He soon met a fellow who was taking
a fat lamb to market.
When the man saw the dog,
he began to weep.

"Oh, he reminds me of my dog
who was lost so long ago,"
said the fellow.
"Would you take this fine lamb for the dog?"
"Of course," said the cat,
and he continued on his way.

Trala lala
I gave my thorn and got some bread.
I lost the bread and gained a hen.
I gave the hen for some nice red yarn.
I traded the yarn for a fine old coat.
I gave the coat to get a dog.
I swapped the dog for a big fat lamb.
Trala

He then saw a sad shepherd by the side of the road
with a staff in one hand and a mandolin over his shoulder.
"What is wrong, my good fellow?" asked the cat.
"Why are you so sad?
With a mandolin like that
you can play music all the long day."

"But that is exactly how I lost my flock,"
said the shepherd.
"And what will I do now?"

"Well," said the cat,
"I have a nice fat lamb with
which you can start again."

The shepherd looked at the lamb
and clapped his hands in delight.
"Your nice fat lamb is about
to have more lambs," he said.
"That won't make a flock,
but it would be a start.
What can I give you in return?"
"I would love to have your mandolin," said the cat,
"for I am a cat who loves to sing."

And so they made the trade and the cat traveled on,
strumming his new mandolin.

Trala lala
I gave my thorn and got some bread.
I lost the bread and gained a hen.
I gave the hen for some nice red yarn.
I traded the yarn for a fine old coat.
I gave the coat to get a dog
and swapped the dog for a nice fat lamb.
I traded the lamb for a mandolin,
and this I will keep to play my songs.
Trala lala lala lala.

CAT SONG

There once was a cat who loved to sing,

Tra lala la la la la.

The cat went a-long and sang his song,

Tra lala la la la la.

Tra la la, la la la, la la la.

There once was a cat who loved to sing

And he sang his whole life long.